How d [barcode] know about the weather?

Contents

Before reading	2
Chapter 1 Weather pictures	6
Chapter 2 Meteorologists	9
Chapter 3 Weather stations	12
Chapter 4 Different weather	16
Mini-dictionary	30
After reading	31

Written by Sally Morgan

Illustrated by Abdi

Collins

What's in this book?

Listen and say

sunny

snow

🎧 ② Charlie and his mother want to go for a walk. Charlie's mum looks at her phone.

"What are you looking at?" asks Charlie.

"I'm looking at today's weather," says Mum.

4

There's a picture on the phone of a black cloud with white **spots** under it.

"What does that picture mean?" asks Charlie.

"It means rain at 2 o'clock, Charlie. Let's put on our coats and boots," says Mum.

"How does your phone know the weather, Mum?" asks Charlie.

Chapter 1 Weather pictures

How do we know what the weather is like today? We can look on our phones or computers to see.

These pictures show the weather. Do you know what they mean? There's a sun, a white cloud, a black cloud with spots of rain and a black cloud with snow. Some pictures show the sun and a cloud. What do you think that means?

Do you know what this picture means?

It means cloudy weather with some sun.
You can go outside and play.

The weather pictures help us decide what to wear and what to do.

In sunny weather, families go to the beach.
People like to swim in the sea. Some people
play ball on the sand or sit in the sun.

People don't want to be on the beach in
the rain!

Chapter 2 Meteorologists

A meteorologist tells us what the weather is like today. Sometimes it's a difficult job.

Meteorologists ask lots of questions about the weather. How hot is it today? Is the wind moving quickly or slowly? Are there lots of clouds in the sky? What colour are they? How big are they? What shape are they?

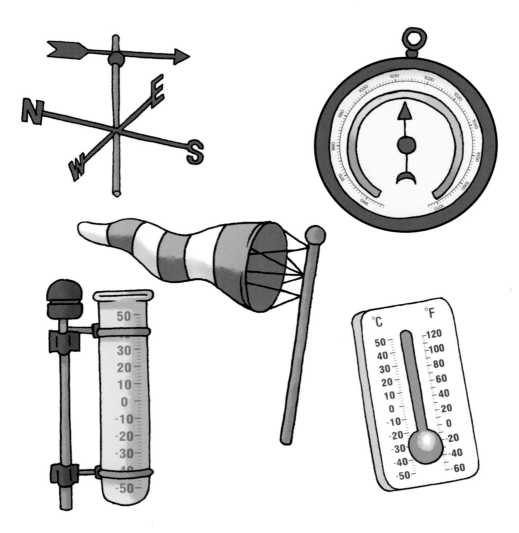

Meteorologists use these things to help them answer these questions.

They are in places called **weather stations**.

Chapter 3 Weather stations

Weather stations can be on the ground, at sea, or up in the sky. They cannot be near trees or buildings.

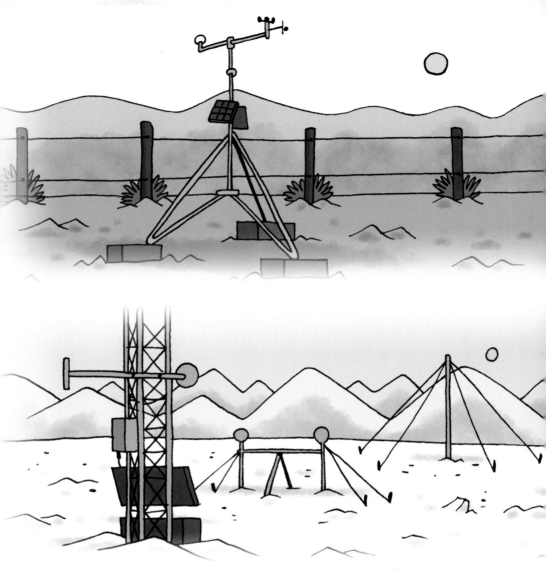

There are weather stations on top of
mountains, in **deserts** and in the snow
and ice. They all tell us about the weather
in those places.

Meteorologists get the information from the weather stations and put it into a computer. The computer helps them know what the weather is like today, this week and this weekend.

Meteorologists tell us what the weather is so we know what to wear and what to do. Often they are right, but sometimes they are wrong.

Chapter 4 Different weather

On a windy day, the **sails** of this boat catch the wind. The wind moves the boat in the water.

Surfers on the waves

You can see waves at the beach. The wind makes the waves. Strong winds make the biggest waves. **Surfers** like to **surf** on the waves.

These are **dark** clouds. Dark clouds carry a lot of water. We see these clouds before there's rain!

These **storm** clouds are very tall and dark. In a storm there's a lot of rain and sometimes it's windy, too. Some storms make a lot of noise. This is called **thunder**. Thunder is very loud.

When there's thunder, there's lightning, too. You can see lightning in the dark sky. You see lightning and then you **hear** the thunder.

Some storms bring lots of rain and wind.
The wind is very strong. It's often difficult for
people to walk around the city. The strong
winds are **dangerous**. Trees can fall in
strong wind.

The biggest storms are called **typhoons**. They are very dangerous.

There's lots of rain. Sometimes the water goes into houses and onto the roads. People try to make their houses safe with bags of sand.

Sometimes cloud falls to the ground. This cloud
is called fog.

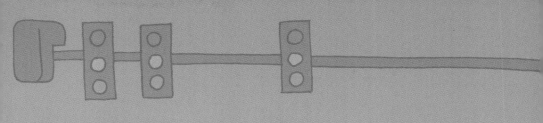

fog

Fog on roads is dangerous because drivers can't see the road. They drive slowly in fog.
When the sun comes again, the fog goes away.

Some people wake up and look out of the window. This is what they see.

There's ice on the grass and trees. This ice is called **frost**. You see frost on cold mornings.

In winter, you can see ice on car windows.
Sometimes there's snow on the ground, too.
Snow is very cold rain. People cannot drive a
car with ice and snow on it. People clean the
windows before they drive. They drive slowly in
snow. They wear big warm clothes, too.

A polar bear in the Arctic

Some places are always very cold. In the Arctic, there's snow on the ground all year. The snow never goes away. It's a white world.
Polar bears live here.

26

Some places are very hot. Jungles are always hot and wet. There's lots of rain.

There are lots of tall trees. Many animals live in the trees. There are birds, monkeys and snakes.

What do you like to do when it's hot and when it's cold?

29

Mini-dictionary

Listen and read

dangerous (adjective) Something that is **dangerous** can hurt or kill someone.

dark (adjective) **Dark** clouds are grey or black. It often rains when there are dark clouds.

desert (noun) A **desert** is an area of land, usually in a hot place, where there's almost no water, rain, trees or plants.

frost (noun) **Frost** is white ice that you can see outside on the ground when the weather is very cold.

hear (verb) When you **hear** a sound, you know about it because it comes to your ears.

meteorologist (noun) A **meteorologist** is someone who tells us what the weather is like.

sail (noun) The **sails** on a boat are the big pieces of cloth that use the wind to move the boat.

spot (noun) A **spot** is a small, round area that you can see on something.

surf (verb) When you **surf**, you ride on big waves in the sea on a special board.

surfer (noun) A **surfer** is someone who likes to ride on big waves in the sea.

storm (noun) A **storm** is very bad weather, when there's rain and strong wind.

thunder (noun) **Thunder** is the loud noise that you sometimes hear from the sky during a storm.

typhoon (noun) A **typhoon** is a really bad storm with a lot of rain and very strong winds.

weather station (noun) A **weather station** is a place where you can find out facts about the weather.

1 Look and match.

fog   frost   hot and sunny   storm   rain

2 Listen and say

Collins

Published by Collins
An imprint of HarperCollins*Publishers*
Westerhill Road
Bishopbriggs
Glasgow
G64 2QT

William Collins' dream of knowledge for all began with the publication of his first book in 1819.

A self-educated mill worker, he not only enriched millions of lives, but also founded a flourishing publishing house. Today, staying true to this spirit, Collins books are packed with inspiration, innovation and practical expertise. They place you at the centre of a world of possibility and give you exactly what you need to explore it.

© HarperCollins*Publishers* Limited 2020

10 9 8 7 6 5 4 3 2 1

ISBN 978-0-00-839751-7

Collins® and COBUILD® are registered trademarks of HarperCollins*Publishers* Limited

www.collins.co.uk/elt

Author: Sally Morgan
Illustrator: Abdi (Beehive)
Series editor: Rebecca Adlard
Commissioning editor: Zoë Clarke
Publishing manager: Lisa Todd
Product managers: Jennifer Hall and Caroline Green
In-house editor: Alma Puts Keren
Project manager: Emily Hooton
Editor: Matthew Hancock
Proofreaders: Natalie Murray and Michael Lamb
Cover designer: Kevin Robbins
Typesetter: 2Hoots Publishing Services Ltd
Audio produced by id audio, London
Reading guide author: Emma Wilkinson
Production controller: Rachel Weaver
Printed and bound by: GPS Group, Slovenia

MIX
Paper from responsible sources
FSC www.fsc.org **FSC™ C007454**

Download the audio for this book and a reading guide for parents and teachers at www.collins.co.uk/839751